GW00356788

I Wish...

Wish poems by John Dean

with illustrations by Erik Sansom

For Judith,
All my best wishes
John Dean

HB
HARVEY BOOKS

I Wish... © 2007 John Dean.
johnmichaeldean@yahoo.co.uk

Published by Harvey Books.
First Edition 2007.

Illustration by Erik Sansom
esansom@sympatico.ca

All rights reserved. No part of this book may be reproduced, stored in a
retrieval system or transmitted in any form by any means (electronic or
mechanical, through reprographic, digital transmission, recording or
otherwise) without the prior written permission of the publisher.

Typeset by Publishing Solutions.
www.publishingsolutions.co.uk

Printed in Spain by MCC Graphics on FSC paper.
www.mccgraphics.co.uk

ISBN 978 0 946988 81 5

For Hope

Contents

From Harvey Books

By the same author:
Stuff and Nonsense.
A book of verse for children,
first published in 2006.

Acknowledgements

Assistance in editing was provided by Victoria Smith,
Lucy Dean, Valerie Maslen and Kevin Inskip.

William Roe suggested that there should be a
poem about the author on the back cover.

I Wish I was a Fat and Slimy Green Revolting Frog
is an adaptation of a poem by Dr John Gamble,
father of one of the author's pupils back in the late seventies.

Introduction

See a star,
May your wish come true —
This is what
I wish for you.

We all have our wishes. Many will never come true, but be not discouraged — wish on, and maybe one day...

Oh, and look for the stars. There is at least one in each illustration.

And please e-mail (using the e-mail address of your parents or guardian) and let me know what you think of the book. Further copies can be ordered from this e-mail address.

I wish you well,

John Dean.
johnmichaeldean@yahoo.co.uk

I Wish...

...For Something Better

I wish for something better –
Please wave your wand at me.
You're a fairy and I need a wish –
That should be plain to see.

The realisation of some minor dream
Must eventually be mine –
I'm not asking to have everything –
One or two things would be fine.

...My Feet weren't Smelly

I wish my feet weren't smelly –
My popularity was in doubt
When I took my shoes off in the alley
And knocked my best mate out.

If I sweated in a fragrant way –
Hints of lavender or rose –
My folks would grab my feet and say,
"Give me a whiff of those!"

...I had a Guinea Pig

I wish I had a guinea pig,
I'd treat it with such care,
I'd take it out on trips with me,
I'd comb its fluffy hair.

I'd tickle it and make it squeak,
I'd feed it till it's fat;
A guinea pig gives pleasure
And I could do with that.

...I was a Fat and Slimy
Green Revolting Frog

I wish I was a fat and slimy
Green revolting frog,
Sitting there upon the edge
Of a black and smelly bog.

I'd laze around from dawn till dusk,
Have mosquitoes for my tea –
But since I'm a human being
I'm afraid that they have me.

...I was a Star

I wish I was a star,
Appearing on TV,
Appearing in the movies –
How brilliant it would be!

And I wouldn't be conceited,
I just want the fame –
To be adored by everyone,
That would be my aim.

...I could eat Chocolate

I wish I could eat chocolate,
But it brings me out in spots.
I could hide away with chocolate,
With lots and lots and lots.

In a world made out of chocolate
One could forgive the odd skin blemish.
I love Belgian chocolate –
O the joy of being Flemish!

...I was an Elephant

I wish I was an elephant,
I would stamp on feet –
The pleasure gained in doing so
Would make my life complete.

And I'd fill my trunk with water
And squirt it at my mum –
And what enormous droppings
I would let out from my bum.

...I was less like my Brothers

I wish I was less like my brothers –
They have little going for 'em –
They lack in looks, in deportment,
In finesse and in decorum.

I wish I was more like my sisters –
Of the princess, of the elf.
All right, my friends would laugh at me,
But I'd feel better in myself.

...I knew my Alphabet

I wish I knew my alphabet –
You know, my ABD –
Other kids I play with
Have known since they were three.

My dad is an optician,
But the alphabet he uses
Is so far away from normal
That I'm afraid it just confuses.

And if I knew my alphabet
It would prove I wasn't dim,
And I could nip into Dad's clinic
And teach it all to him.

...I was a Hedgehog

I wish I was a hedgehog –
They're sweet, but with defence –
Such a combination of attributes
Can make for perfect sense.

I could act all cute and let people stroke
My snout – but then, quite quickly,
I could roll up tight into a ball
And make myself all prickly.

... I was more Purposeful

I wish I was more purposeful,
I stand around and slouch –
My fur is all dishevelled,
I keep a messy pouch.

For a kangaroo I'm lazy,
I loaf around all week –
Every other kangaroo
Is workmanlike and sleek.

...I was a Dinosaur

I wish I was a dinosaur –
O such should be my fate! –
I'd live out in the garden,
It really would be great.

I would need to be a meat eater –
I couldn't live on veg –
But I suppose, just as a starter,
I could gobble up the hedge.

...I had Pyjamas

I wish I had pyjamas
And not just pants and vest –
In a pair of flannelettes
My parents should invest.

"We can't afford such luxuries,"
I heard father say to mother –
But they have no problem keeping warm
Since they have got each other.

...I had a Fox's Tail

I wish I had a fox's tail,
I could stroke it when I'm tense –
Or a prehensile tail to help me climb
Up tree or wall or fence.

A peacock's tail would be fun
With all those looming eyes –
Even with a horse's tail
I could swish away the flies.

And I'd look cute with a squirrel's tail
Sprouting from behind –
I wish a tail for everyone,
The whole of human kind.

...I was a Planet

I wish I was a planet,
I would not let me die,
I'd take good care of my environment,
I'd wear a Greenpeace tie.

I'd dispose of my pollution,
I'd put it into space,
And turn it into giant signs
To warn the human race.

...I had Six Brothers and Six Sisters

I wish I had six brothers
And six sisters on my shelves
And that they did unto others
What they would do unto themselves.

It would end my lonely scribbling –
O how nice the world would be! –
With many an extra sibling
Being nice to me!

...I could be Scottish

I wish I could be Scottish,
They have so much fun up there –
Their country is so beautiful,
They breathe such fresh clean air.

With monsters in their lochs
They bellow, "Auld Lang Syne!"
If I was only Scottish –
So much pleasure would be mine.

And I love the Scottish accent –
Yes, when you are born a Scot
You must be so delighted
With everything you've got.

With a sporran on my kilt
And a haggis in my hand
I'd stand upon Ben Nevis
And smile upon the land.

...I was a Mantelpiece

I wish I was a mantelpiece,
My friends could lean on me,
And in the winter when the fire's on
How cosy I would be.

I could display my birthday cards
And keep them there for days –
Yes, this is an actual wish of mine
And not some silly phase.

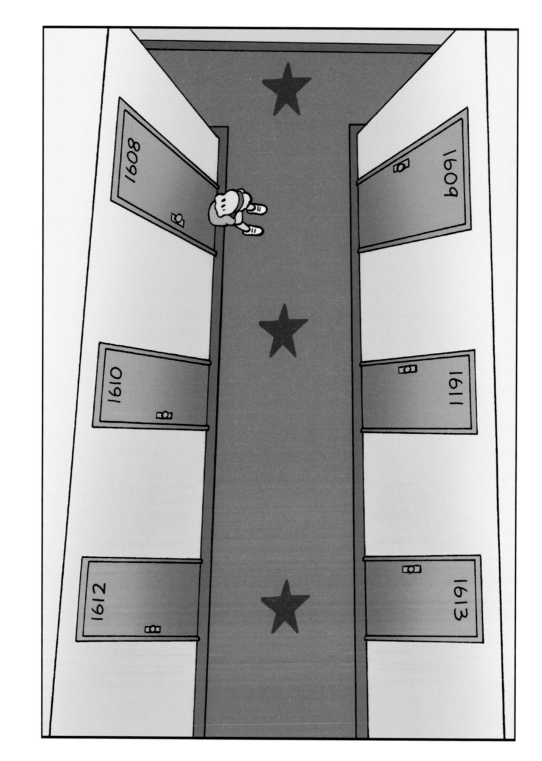

...I had a Pony

I wish I had a pony,
I'd ride it every day –
At night, to make it cosy,
I'd give it tons of hay.

Mum says that in our block of flats
It would be a silly gift –
Well, if it couldn't manage all those stairs
I could take it in the lift.

If my parents bought a pony
I would love them till I die,
But they won't buy a pony
So here I sit and cry.

... I was a Robot

I wish I was a robot
And if you ask me why –
Well, without water in its workings
A robot cannot cry.

And if I was a robot
I'd fight to make things right –
I'd creep up on my bullies
And give them such a fright.

...I was a Meerkat

I wish I was a meerkat,
All long and thin and sweet,
With staring eyes, a worried look
And tiny little feet.

And if I was a meerkat
I'd play "watch" throughout the day
High up on the highest ground
Muttering away –

Standing on my back legs
With my front legs hanging down –
And all I'd need to gain perfection
Would be a golden crown.

...I had a Propeller

I wish I had a propeller,
I'd zoom up in the air –
I haven't got a pair of wings
So a propeller's only fair.

At bath time I would dip myself
Beginning at my feet –
And once finished the propeller
Would dry me off a treat.

I wouldn't have to hurry,
I could laze around in bed –
Then go whizzing down the stairs
And, still in flight, get fed.

At school I could escape PE,
Assemblies and detention –
And pull faces at the teachers
Without fear of intervention.

...I was one of the Boys

I wish I was one of the boys
Instead of just one of the girls –
I'm fed up with ponies and pigtails
And delicate meaningless twirls.

I want to be out in the dirt and the muck,
To tussle and wrestle and fight –
Coming home all covered in bruises
Would fill me with utter delight.

...I could do Origami

I wish I could do origami,
Winter evenings would be fun –
I could create amazing things
For me and everyone.

People would be in awe of me
If I had the gift, if only –
A magazine to a moose,
A pamphlet to a pony –

A newspaper to a skyscraper,
An encyclopaedia into me –
What a treasure chest of wonder
Our living room would be.

...I was a Starfish

I wish I was a starfish
Walking in the sea,
Coming out and sticking
To my silly sister's knee.

My consideration of the starfish:
It is perfect, but it's odd –
The strangest living creature
Ever made by God.

...I had a Dodo

I wish I had a dodo,
So peculiar, yet alluring;
It would be the only one and so
My fame would be enduring.

If you don't know the dodo,
And let's pretend I'm one,
The only living dodo
That walks beneath the Sun –

I died out many years ago
On the island of Mauritius –
There were hungry sailors then, you know,
And I was most delicious.

But now I live in Woking
And I go along to shows
And people are all for stroking
My big and beaky nose.

All plump and dim my life's a breeze –
I won't let fate defeat me –
And I do forgive the Portuguese –
They had their reasons, then, to eat me.

...I was a Gorilla

I wish I was a gorilla,
I love the way they act –
I'd beat my chest and roar at folks
Without an ounce of tact.

What you'd see is what you'd get –
A great big hunky beast.
I'd not give up my skiing, though –
You'd still see me on the piste.

...I lived in a Bouncy Castle

I wish I lived in a bouncy castle
Instead of a basement flat,
With a bouncy bath and a bouncy bed
And a bouncy clawless cat.

I'd bounce up and down the stairs
In a double twist and pike –
Yes, to live in a bouncy castle
Is exactly what I'd like.

...I had Hypnotic Powers

I wish I had hypnotic powers,
People would obey me,
Everyone would be my friend
And no one would betray me.

If I had hypnotic powers
Nasty people would be good.
Give me hypnotic powers! –
Come on, you know you should!

...You'd wish for an Extra Arm

I wish you'd wish for an extra arm –
It's great as you can see –
When I'm carrying a heavy weight
It holds the door for me.

Juggling is easy now
And I play some awkward pieces
On the drums and the piano –
O the potential it releases!

When I'm climbing and I get an itch
That third arm is needed –
In all things that are dextrous
I am never now impeded.

I believe that extra arms
Should be genetically provided –
So, come on, don't waste a wish –
Use it here, like I did!

...I was an Aardvark

I wish I was an aardvark,
But not a porcupine,
And not a duck-billed platypus –
No, an aardvark would be fine.

I'd be top of every list,
I'd have termites for my tea –
Yes, nothing but the best in life
Would lend itself to me.

...I could have a Nose Job

I wish I could have a nose job –
Mine's an enormous snout –
It must have such a root in it
Because I can't pull it out.

A tiny nose is beautiful,
That is my assertion,
So perhaps they could replace my one
With the smallest version.

...I was a Mantis

I wish I was a mantis,
Then when I'm out late playing
If my parents call me in
I could pretend that I am praying.

And when I'm better at it
I could act just like a stick –
I could stay out all night long
Once I have learned this trick.

...My Brother had a Tiny Head

I wish my brother had a tiny head –
He thinks he knows it all –
He could not be a big head –
Not if his head was small.

Maybe then when we play games
I would not be defeated –
Yes, it would be nice to have a brother
Who was not quite so conceited.

...I was a Ballerina

I wish I was a ballerina,
I'd fly in through the door,
I'd tip-toe in my tutu
And glide across the floor.

The ballerina is pretty,
Delightful and petite –
From the top of her tiara
To her little pointed feet.

To be a ballerina would
Fill me with such joy,
But it is difficult when I
Am a great big clumsy boy.

...I was a Genie

I wish I was a genie
Living in a lamp –
I know I'd be all huddled up
And I'd probably get cramp –

But away from this troubled world
I could gain release,
Sitting with my knitting
In my tiny little niche –

Rays of gentle sunshine
Shining through my sprout,
And I'd always have two wishes
If I needed to get out.

...I could be Zany

I wish I could be zany,
I'm such a boring lad,
I stay in when it's rainy,
I'm never raving mad.

I ought to run around
With nothing on my feet,
To beat upon the ground
And call out, "Tweet! Tweet! Tweet!" –

Hang bobbles from my hair,
Mimic what folks say,
But I'd have to take good care
Or I might get locked away.

...I was a Composer

I wish I was a composer,
Like Johannes Brahms –
People would stop me in the street
And take me in their arms.

Life for me would be a treat
With a great big ribbon tied on,
Especially if I could write as much
As good old F.J.Haydn.

...I was a Lunchbox

I wish I was a lunchbox,
Like that one on the shelf –
But then all the food within me
I'd keep it for myself.

And every time my owner tried
To take it from my tummy
I'd trap her fingers and off she'd go
Crying to her mummy.

...I was a Crocodile

I wish I was a crocodile,
All ill-tempered and snappy –
No longer would I have to smile
And pretend that I am happy.

O to do the things I can't! –
To be wholly indiscreet! –
To chase away my boring aunt
And bite her on the feet.

...I was a Cactus

I wish I was a cactus,
No one on Earth to harm me –
If I came across a lion
It would not alarm me.

I wouldn't have to work –
No job needs a plant –
And if someone asked me for a hand
I'd simply say, "I can't!"

So with little expected of me
I could laze around in bed –
Yes, for the wish to be a cactus
There is something to be said.

...I had Three Wishes

I wish I had three wishes,
But there goes one already –
If I am not to waste them all
I had better take it steady.

I just wish I knew what I would want –
Oh, no! That's number two!
I wish I could stop doing this! –
Oh dear!
That's that!
I'm through!

Wish List